The sun was up, but
it was not hot.

Don had a rod and Lil had a rod.

A man had a cat on
his tug.

Lil and Don ran to
get on the tug.

The man had a big net.

Don got a tug on
his rod.
The cat sat up.

Don had to tug, but it was a lot of fun.

Lil had a rod and the man had a net.

Lil got a big tug on
the rod.

Lil had to tug on it.
It was a big job to
get a cod.

Lil got wet, but
Lil got the cod.

The man got the
cod from Lil.
The cod hit the cat.
The cat ran.

The man set the
cod in a big tub.
The cat ran up to
the tub.

Lil and Don sat and
had a can of pop.

Lil and Don ran
to get the cod.
But the cod was
not in the tub.

The cat sat in the tub,
and the cat was fat.

Is it fun to get wet?

Del got the dog wet.

Del got the cat wet.

The cat was sad.

The cat ran.

Del ran up to Jon.

Del got Jon wet.

Jon was mad.

Del ran.

Jon ran to get Del.

Del ran up to Viv.

Del got Viv wet.

Viv was mad at Del.

Viv ran to get Del.

The dog was mad at
Del.
The cat was mad at
Del.

Jon was mad at Del.
And Viv was mad at
Del.

Del hit a big tub.

Del fell.

Del was in the tub.
It was wet in the big
tub.

Del was wet and sad.
It was not fun to get
wet.

Gum is fun.

Gus can get gum.

Gus had a lot of gum.
A lot of gum is a lot
of fun.

Gus can pop his gum.
It is fun to pop gum.

Gus was sad.

The gum got on him.

The gum got on his lip.
And it got on his cap.

The cat ran to hop

up on Gus.

The cat got in his lap.

The gum got big.

The cat hit the gum.

The cat got the gum
to pop.

The cat can not get
rid of the gum.

Gus had to rub to
get rid of the gum.

Gus had to cut to
get rid of the gum.

Gus was sad.

And the cat was sad.

Gus got rid of the
gum on his cat.

Gum is fun, but not

on a cat.

The cat ran.

Sam had a nap.

In the nap, Sam
ran a cab.

A cat had a hat.

The cat sat in the cab.

A rat had a map.

The rat sat in the cab.

Where is Sam's hat?

The man sat in the cab.

The ram had a bat.

The ram sat in the cab.

Was Sam in the cab?

Sam had a bad nap.

Kim can dig.
Wag can dig.

Wag did dig in
Kim's hill.
Kim was mad at Wag.

Wag ran.

Kim ran to Wag.

Kim can dig a hill
for Wag.

Wag can dig in the hill.

Wag can sit at the hill.

Wag can sit in the hill.

Where is Wag?

Kim was rid of Wag.

Kim can dig.

Kim did miss Wag.

Kim was sad.
Wag was a pal.

Kim ran to Wag's hill.

Where was Wag?

Wag was in the hill!

Kim and Wag will dig
in the hill.

Sid was big.
Tod was not as big
as Sid.

Sid had a big van.

"Sid the Kid" was in

his van.

Tod had a hot rod.
"Tod the Hot Rod" was
in his hot rod.

Sid had a cat.
The cat had a nap
on top of the van.

Tod had his dog in the hot rod.

The hot rod hit the van.

Sid was in the van.

Sid was mad at Tod.

The cat was mad.

Tod and his dog hid.

Tod was in a jam.
Sid was mad at him.

Tod got in.

Then Sid got the hot rod.

Sid had Tod and the hot rod in a big lot.

The hot rod can not hit the van if it is in the lot.

The hot rod can not

ram the van.

Tod sat in his hot rod.

His dog got in the hot rod.

Sid ran to hop in
his van.

Sid got a rag and got

to his job.

The cat had a nap on

top of the van.

The van was in a rut.

The van was up to its hub cap in mud.

The man dug in the mud.

The van was not in the rut.

But the man had mud on him.

The mud was a lot of fun to the pup.

The van hit the mud.

The mud got on Pam.

The mud was a lot of fun to the pup.

The cab hit the mud.

The mud got on

the cat.

The mud was a lot of fun to the pup.

The bus hit the mud.

The mud got on the pup.

The mud was fun
on a man.
The mud was fun
on Pam.

Mud was fun on a cat,

but not on a pup.

Hal has a dog.
Nip is his dog.

Nip is a lot of fun.

Nip can hop up on

Hal's bed.

Nip has a lot of pep.

He got mud on the bed.

Nip and Hal hid.

Hal and Nip run in
the sun.
It is fun to run.

Hal let Nip run.
The dog runs and
runs.

Nip got hit.

Tom's big van hit him.

Hal is sad.
His dog can not
get up.

Tom set Nip in
his van.
Hal got in.

Hal and Tom got
Nip to the vet.

The vet set the dog's leg.

Nip got up.

His leg was set.

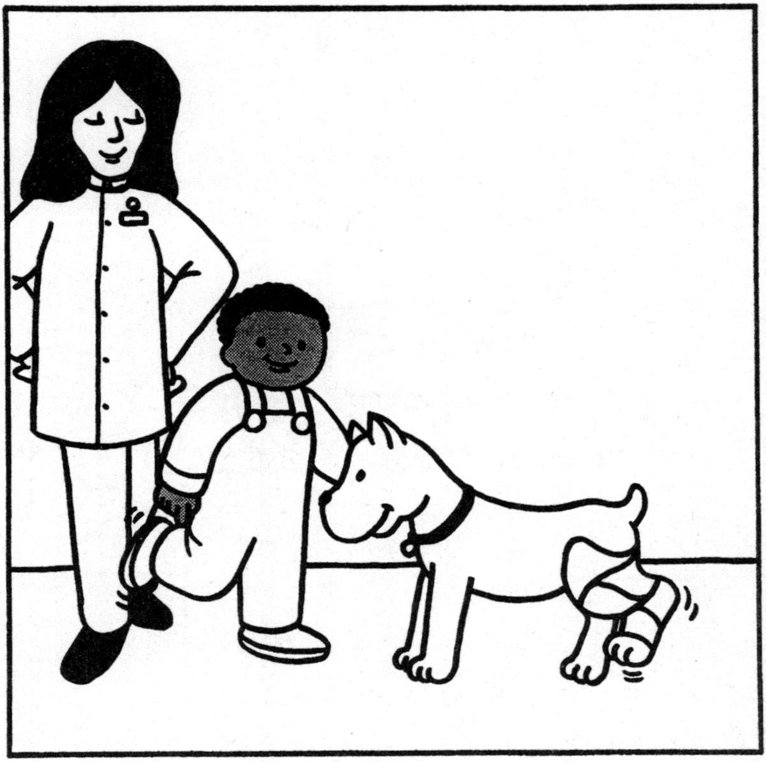

Nip had to hop.

Hal and Tom got in the big van.

Hal had Nip on
his lap.

Nip sat on the rug.

Nip is not sad.

Nip can not run, but

Nip can wag and

wag.

Cop Cat was a cop.
Cop Cat had a big
hat.

Cop Cat had to get
Bad Sam and The Kid.
It was his job.

His hat did not fit him.
The hat was too big.

The Kid ran up to a
man.
The Kid can rob the
man.

Cop Cat ran to get
The Kid.

Cop Cat had his
hat on.
It was too big.
He did not see The Kid.

The Kid ran on.

Cop Cat ran to get him.
As Cop Cat ran to get
him, he fell and got
wet.

The Kid ran on.
Cop Cat got his hat up
and ran to get him.

His hat fell down.
Cop Cat did not see
the log.
He hit it.

Cop Cat got his hat up and ran to get The Kid.

Cop Cat ran to get up.
Cop Cat had to get
The Kid.

Cop Cat did not get up.

He fell.

But he was on top of

The Kid.

A lot of men ran to get The Kid.

A man got Cop Cat up and got him his hat.

Cop Cat had his hat up.
It was a big job to get
The Kid.

Val had a pup.
The pup was Ned.

Ned ran and ran.
Ned had a lot of fun.

It got hot in the sun.
Ned ran to his pan.

Ned got in his pan
to get a sip.

Ned got wet.

Val had to get a mop.

Ned got up and ran.
The pup ran a lot.

The pup had a lot of
pep.
It was fun to run.

It got hot in the sun.
Ned ran to his pan.

Ned got in the pan

to get a sip.

Ned got wet.

Val had to get the mop.

The pup ran and ran.
The pup had a lot of
pep.

It got hot in the sun.
Ned ran to his pan.

Val ran and got him.
Ned did not get to
his pan.

Val set Ned in a
big tub.
Ned had fun in the
tub.

It was fun to get wet,

but not fun to mop

up.

Val and Ned had a lot of fun in the tub in the sun.